Chapter One

The king was very old. It was time for somebody else to take his place. But he had a problem. A big problem. He did not have any children. So what could he do?

The king sat for many nights trying to think of an answer. It was impossible.

Finally, he called together all the wise people of the land. Maybe they could help him?

After lots of talking, an old woman came forward.

"Your Majesty!" she said. "We have thought very hard about your problem. The answer is simple."

"Oh good!" said the king. "Tell me more..."

"You must give flower seeds to every person in the land," said the old woman. "Whoever grows the best flower shall be the next king or queen!"

"But that's silly," said the king. "Anyone can grow flowers!"

"Maybe, maybe not..." said the old woman. Then she bent over and whispered something in his ear.

"You *are* clever," smiled the king. "We must send out the seeds at once!"

Chapter Two

The king ordered a thousand sacks of very special flower seeds. His servants put them into small paper packets.

After a week, there were a million packets of seeds. Enough for every house in the land.

The servants rode across the hills in every direction – north, south, east and west – to deliver the seeds.

Every packet came with a message:

The king is old and wishes to retire. He wants to pass on his kingdom but he does not have any children. These seeds are the answer to his problem. Whoever grows the best flowers within three weeks shall be ruler of all this land!

As the seeds landed on doorsteps, villagers and townspeople gathered to gossip.

"The king's gone a bit bonkers!"

"But think of all the gold and jewels!"

"You could stuff your face with fancy food!"

"And have fun ordering people about all day!"

Everyone greedily grabbed their seeds. They planted them in pots and began to dream big, flowery dreams.

Chapter Three

Jack did not have time for big, flowery dreams. He spent all day working...

and all night looking after his sick mother.

One evening, after a meal of cold potatoes, Jack heard the sound of horses' hooves coming down the lane. A moment later, a packet was pushed under the door.

Jack picked it up and read out the
message.

"This must be a joke!" he said.
Jack's mother took the letter. She
pointed to the bottom of the page.
"Look. There's the royal seal. This
comes from the king himself!"

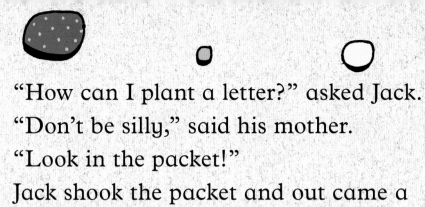

"How can I plant a letter?" asked Jack.
"Don't be silly," said his mother.
"Look in the packet!"
Jack shook the packet and out came a
handful of tiny seeds.

17

"I don't have a chance!" he said, shaking his head. "The day I become king will be the day the sun says hello to the moon!"

Chapter Four

That evening, Jack helped his mother into a chair by the fire and put a blanket over her knees.

"You're a good boy, Jack," she said. "Now, what are you going to do about these?" She pointed at the packet of seeds.

Jack thought for a moment.
"Plant them, of course! Even if I don't
win, the flowers will cheer you up!"

Jack found an old clay pot and filled it with soil. He made holes with his fingers and pushed the seeds deep down.

He fetched water from the well and wet
the soil.

He put the pot by the window to soak
up the sun.

A week went by.

"Can you see anything yet?" his mother asked.

"No," said Jack, glumly.

He took the pot outside and placed it in a sunny spot.

A week went by.

"Can you see anything yet?" his mother asked.

"No," said Jack, very glumly.

Time was running out. He sang songs to his seeds.

A week went by.

"Can you see anything *yet*?" his mother asked.

"No," said Jack, even more glumly. He did not know what to do. The three weeks were up. Tomorrow, the king was judging the flowers and Jack had nothing to show.

Chapter Five

In the morning, Jack walked into the city carrying his empty pot. The queue outside the palace stretched for miles.

Jack was right at the back. Every
person in front was holding a pot full
of amazing flowers.

There were:
Sweet Peas and Poppies

Cowslips and Cornflowers

Foxgloves and Forget-Me-Nots

Sunflowers and Stocks

Daisies and Busy Lizzies

Marigolds and Morning Glories

And many more beside.

Finally, as the sun was setting, Jack stood before the king. He told his sad story.

"Your Majesty, I did my best. I watered the seeds and put them in the sun. I even tried singing to them, but still they would not grow."

The king was not cross. Instead, he smiled.

"Dear Jack. Don't be sad. Every seed I handed out was as dead as a sausage. Every flower you see was grown by a liar! You are the only honest person in the land, so... you shall be the next king!"

And from that day, Jack looked after both his mother *and* the kingdom. Of course, Jack was very good at being king, so everyone was very happy.

And the moral of the tale? In the end, honesty pays very well indeed!